LEGENDS
(in their own lunchbox)

Chaz and the Missing Mayo

James Roy & Dean Gorissen

capstone
classroom

Legends (in Their Own Lunchbox) is published by Capstone Classroom
1710 Roe Crest Drive
North Mankato, MN 56003
www.capstoneclassroom.com

Library of Congress Cataloging-In-Publication data is available on the Library of
Congress website.

ISBN: 978-1-4966-0245-9

This edition of *Chaz and the Missing Mayo* is published by arrangement with Macmillan
Publishers Australia Pty Ltd 2013.

Photo credits: iStockphoto.com/marlanu, **44**

This book has been officially leveled by using the F&P Text Level Gradient™
Leveling System.

Printed in China

Contents

MEET the Characters

I'm Chaz.
I love cooking,
though not
everyone loves
my dishes!

I'm Toby, Chaz's official food taster. Unfortunately for me...

I'm Toby's mom. Life is never boring when Chaz comes over.

Chapter 1

Boring Veggie Sandwiches

Chaz turned up his nose. "A veggie sandwich? Veggie sandwiches are so boring! Don't you have anything else?"

Toby shook his head. "Mom said to have veggie sandwiches."

"Or we could take a walk and get some hamburgers," Chaz suggested.

Toby looked out the window. "It's pouring," he said.

Chaz sighed. "Fine, we'll make boring old sandwiches. Is this the bread we're using? It's whole wheat."

"Mom says whole wheat bread is better for you," Toby said. He opened the fridge and looked inside. "Lettuce, tomatoes, and cucumber."

He put them on the counter beside the bread. "Is that all we need?"

"How about butter? How about cheese?"

"Good idea," said Toby.

He took out the butter and the cheese and put them on the counter with the other things. "Is that everything?"

"How about mayonnaise?" said Chaz. "You can't have a veggie sandwich without mayo."

"I don't think we have any," said Toby.

"Let me look." Chaz opened the fridge door and peered inside.

First he looked on the top shelf.

No mayo.

Then he looked on the middle shelf.

No mayo.

He looked on the bottom shelf, and on the little shelves in the door.

No mayo anywhere.

"Nope, there's no mayonnaise," he said.

"I told you," said Toby. "I guess we'll just have to do without."

"No! No, that's not good enough!" Chaz said. "You *can't* have a veggie sandwich without mayo! You just can't! It'll be *too* boring. We should walk down to Mr. Santo's store and buy some."

"I already told you, it's raining."
That was when Chaz had one of
his amazing ideas. "Yes!" he said with
wide eyes and an even wider grin.

"What?" said Toby, looking a lot less excited than Chaz.

"We'll make our own!"

Chapter 2

The Prep

"How can we make our own mayonnaise?" Toby asked. "Mayo comes in a jar."

"It'll be easy," Chaz said. "All the top chefs make their own mayo."

"Easy?" Toby repeated.

"Well, maybe not for you, but definitely for me. All I need is a recipe!" Chaz pointed at all the cookbooks lined up along the kitchen shelf. "There has to be a recipe for mayo in one of those books."

"Maybe," said Toby.

They took down a big stack of cookbooks and started searching. After about five minutes, Toby said, "I think I found it! 'A simple recipe for making fresh mayonnaise.'"

"Awesome!" said Chaz. "What's in the recipe?"

"See for yourself," Toby said, handing Chaz the cookbook.

Homemade Mayonnaise

You'll need:

4 medium-sized eggs

1 cup of olive oil

1 tablespoon of lemon juice

"That's easy!" said Chaz.
"We can make it! Well, I can make
it, and you can be my apprentice.
You can help me with my prep."

"Oh, thanks," said Toby.

"You're welcome. This'll be fun!
It'll be like *Superchef* on TV!
Do we have eggs? Quick, look!"

Toby opened the fridge and checked the shelves one by one. "Nope, no eggs," he said after a while.

"Maybe they're in the pantry," Chaz suggested.

Toby frowned and closed the fridge. "Eggs in the pantry?"

Chaz shrugged. "Sometimes things get put back in the wrong place. I'll look."

"Okay," said Toby. "But I'm getting pretty hungry. Maybe I'll just make a plain sandwich."

"No!" said Chaz, slapping his hand on the counter. "No, this is going to be amazing! Amazing, I say! Let me check in the pantry. Please?"

"Fine," said Toby. "But if you don't find any eggs, I'm just going to go ahead without the mayo."

Chapter 3

Chef and Apprentice

There was a lot of food in the pantry. There were jars and cans and packets. There were plastic containers and boxes and bags of almost everything else you could think of. But there were no eggs.

"We had bacon and eggs for breakfast," said Toby. "Mom must have used up all the eggs."

"No!" said Chaz. "We have to find eggs! We have to make proper mayo! Wait — what's this?" At the back of one of the shelves he'd seen a large plastic egg. It was much bigger than most eggs, and there was a label around it.

He showed the egg to Toby. "Look!" he said.

Toby shook his head. "That won't work. It's not a real egg."

Chaz read the label. "It says here that it's made of powdered egg whites and sugar." He shrugged. "Our mayo will be a little sweet, but we like sweet things, don't we?"

"I guess so."

"Good." Chaz put the plastic egg on the counter next to the butter. "So, what's next?"

Toby frowned at Chaz before looking down at the book again. "One cup of olive oil."

Chaz opened the pantry again. He couldn't find any olive oil, but

when he checked in the fridge he saw
a jar of olives. They were green, and
floating in some watery stuff.

"I don't think that's olive oil," Toby said.

"It's runny like oil," Chaz replied. "Plus it's in the jar with the olives, so it should taste right."

"I don't think so," said Toby.

"Trust me! I'm good at this stuff, remember?"

"Hmm," Toby replied.

"I am! I watch *Superchef* every night. Do you?"

"No," Toby admitted.

"Exactly. So, next is lemon juice. Do we have that?"

"How would I know? You're the expert," Toby said.

Chaz searched everywhere for lemons. He looked in the pantry. He looked in the fruit bowl.

He went to the fridge *again*, but the only thing he could find in there was a bottle of orange juice.

"Oranges and lemons aren't the same thing," Toby said.

"They're both citrus fruit." Chaz took the orange juice and plunked it on the counter. "There — we're ready! Get me a mixing bowl and let's begin! And when I tell you to do something, you have to say 'Yes, Chef!'"

"Yes, Chef."

Chapter 4

Mayo Magic

"I really don't think this is a good idea," said Toby.

"No, because it's a *great* idea!" Chaz opened the plastic egg. Inside was a silver packet and a piece of paper that explained how to make meringues.

Chaz crumpled the paper up and handed it to Toby. "Throw that away. I'm not making meringues — I'm making mayo."

"Hang on," said Toby. "The recipe says we need four eggs. That's only one."

"I know, but it's one *big* egg instead of four *medium* eggs. It'll be fine. Trust me."

Chaz tore open the silver packet. Some white powder spilled onto the counter. He poured the rest into the bowl. "Done. What's next?"

"Olive oil," said Toby. "One cup of olive oil."

"Open the jar of olives, please."

"I *hate* olives," Toby said. "They make me want to be sick."

"You'll be fine," Chaz said. "Hurry, open the jar!"

"Yes, Chef." Toby twisted the lid off the jar. "Oh, the smell ..." he said. Then he started making some horrible gurgling noises in his throat.

Chaz rolled his eyes. "Give it to me. I don't want you to be sick everywhere."

He took the jar of olives and poured the watery stuff into a cup. The cup was only half full. "Do you have any other oil in the kitchen?"

Toby was still trying not to throw up. "There's some oil still in the frying pan from breakfast," he said in a choking voice. "It's got bits of bacon in it."

"We can use that," Chaz said.

"Are you sure?"

"Trust me, I know what I'm doing!"

Chaz added the oil from the frying pan to the green olive-water in the cup.

Then he poured it all onto the white powder in the bowl and stirred it with a spoon.

Toby seemed to be feeling better again. "That looks awful," he said. "It's like a paste. A really lumpy paste."

"I can get the lumps out later," said Chaz.

"Isn't mayo supposed to be white?" said Toby. "That's green, and it has chunks in it! It smells really yucky, too."

"I guess it needs the juice," Chaz suggested. "*Then* it'll be like real mayo. Hurry, I need a tablespoon of lemon juice."

"Orange juice," said Toby.

"Right, orange juice."

"Yes, Chef." Toby found a tablespoon in one of the drawers and measured out the orange juice.

He tipped it into the bowl, and Chaz stirred some more.

"Ew," said Toby. "Now it's turning brown. Chaz, that doesn't look anything like mayo."

"Hmm," said Chaz.

"It doesn't smell anything like mayo, either."

"Hmm. But I bet it tastes like mayo," Chaz said, dipping his finger into the brown, lumpy stuff. "It has to."

Then he opened his mouth and took a deep breath.

Chapter 5

The Taste Test

Chaz's finger was almost in his mouth when Toby's mom walked in. "Oh, you've been busy!" she said. "Boys, before you finish making your lunch, could you do a quick job for me? Could you get the bags of shopping

out of the car for me, please?"

It was still raining, so Chaz and
Toby ran to the car, grabbed the four
bags of groceries, and ran back inside.

They got back just in time to hear
Toby's mom say, "This all looks so
healthy! Whole wheat bread! Veggies!
Cheese! Lovely!"

Then Chaz saw her scoop up a huge
dollop of the icky, brown, lumpy
mess from the bowl on the counter.

It hung on the end of the spoon like a blob of slime. A couple of bits of bacon and burned egg hung trembling from the end.

"Um ... Mom," said Toby.

"And you've been making hummus? I *love* hummus!" she said.

"Mom, I really wouldn't eat that. It's actually—"

But it was too late. She opened her mouth wide and took a great big mouthful.

Then she spit it out all over the counter.

Chaz's Email

From: chaz@litols.com
To: mario@litols.com
Sent: Monday, May 15
Subject: Making Mayo

Hi Mario,

Have you learned any new skateboard tricks
yet? I've been really getting into my cooking.
Last week I made the perfect mayonnaise.
I can't understand why no one else liked it.
So what if I changed a few of the ingredients?
Oil is oil, isn't it? Even when it still has bits of
leftover bacon and egg in it. Here's a picture
of me making my mayo.
Doesn't it look yummy!

Laters,
Chaz

MORE LEGENDS!

Want to find out about my next Superchef adventure? Read my next book! Here's what happens...

LEGENDS (in their own lunchbox)

Chaz at the Fish Market

James Roy & Dean Gorissen

Chaz is on a school trip to the fish market. He loves seafood and there's plenty here, including lots of fish guts and heads! He wasn't planning on getting quite so close up, though ...

Meet the Author

Some good things about James Roy's childhood: getting to grow up in exciting places like Fiji and Papua New Guinea, owning as many books as he could possibly read, having the world's biggest banyan tree in his back yard, and getting pretend-shipwrecked from time to time. Some bad things: falling out of the world's biggest banyan tree, and almost getting shipwrecked for real. Find out more at: www.jamesroy.com.au.

Meet the Illustrator

Dean Gorissen has illustrated a number of
picture books, as well as writing his own.
He began his drawing career specializing
in cowboys and ducks, then moved on to
spaceships and astronauts. He now illustrates,
writes, and designs for lots of people all
over the place.

Read all the books in Set 1